Who Wants to Teach Their Child, History?

Who Wants to Teach Their Child, History?

By

Syed Makhdoom Ali

Gullybaba Publishing House Pvt. Ltd

2525/193, 1st Floor, Old Bus Stand, Opposite Street of Asha
Maternity Center, Tri Nagar, Delhi-110035
Tel.: 27387998, e-mail: info@gullybaba.com
Website: www.GullyBaba.com
www.enhanceyourchild.com

Who Wants to Teach Their Child, History?

by *Syed Makhdoom Ali*

Edition: 2012
Price: Rs. 140/-

ISBN: 978-93-81970-03-4

Dedicated
**to all the parents who wanted to enhance their
children...**

Foreword

Just as having no personal memory deprives us of a sense of our own identity, having no historical memory deprives us of a sense of our national identity. Knowledge of India's history enables us to understand our nation's traditions, its conflicts, and its central ideas, values and organizing principles. Knowledge of world history enables us to understand other cultures. In addition, without historical memory, we miss a great source of enjoyment that comes from piecing together the story of the past — our own, our nation's and the world's. Our historical memory is enriched by our understanding of geography, which lets us better see the physical context of cultures and environments around the world and across time.

By showing interest in their children's education, parents can spark enthusiasm in them and lead them to a very important understanding — that learning can be enjoyable as well as rewarding and is well worth the effort required.

We hope that you find **'Who Wants to Teach Their Child, History?'** a valuable tool for developing and reinforcing your child's interest in and knowledge of history.

Few Words

It is a sad fact that many of the elementary school children in India do not like to study history. A child in third grade complains to his parents about history as a "boring subject." Another felt that there is no use in studying about people and events of past. But it is a wrong notion that undervalues the studies of history. There is no doubt that the primary purpose of schooling is to prepare students to function effectively in the world, and thereby to assist society to function effectively as well. We study the past in school not because students need to know a collection of old facts, but because history helps them understand how the world works and how human beings behave. Knowledge of the past is required for understanding present realities. When people share some common knowledge of history, they can discuss their understandings with one another.

Teaching history in schools/home can be and should be made more interesting than other subjects. Children like stories. It can carve out the future of humanity from its past experiences. It should be made a part of their life experiences. Historical knowledge about their family, their surroundings, etc. can keep history alive. Collecting pictures, coins, etc. can kindle the historical curiosity in children. Part of their joy comes from visiting foreign mental landscapes, part from discovering new things about themselves and a big part is simply the love of a good story. For those with an historical turn of mind, history supplies an endless source of fascination.

This work will provide a helping hand to parents who are in need to understand their adolescent.

- Author

Acknowledgement

I owe a great deal of credit to the many teachers, parents, and children I have visited and interacted. The insight I gain from teachers and learners profoundly influence my understanding of how children successfully learn and act.

First of all I am especially thankful for the support of my wife Khalida and daughter Mahin.

I also wish to express my gratitude to our reviewers for this book: Mr. Dinesh Veerma and Mr. Mahesh Chand.

I am deeply grateful to the Publisher and the staff (GullyBaba Publishing House Pvt. Ltd.) for their excellent work.

And finally for those who have reacted to my evolving ideas have offered many hints for improvement. I appreciate their wisdom and advice.

- **Syed Makhdoom Ali**

Contents

Foreword   *vii*
Few Words   *ix*
Acknowledgement   *xi*

1. Introduction   **1**
  • History Habits • Enjoying History with Your Child
  • How to Use This Book?

2. Some Basics   **7**
  • What is History? • A New Look at the Study of History
  • Geography: An Important Tool for Learning and
  • Understanding History

3. Activities   **13**

4. History as Story   **15**
  • Listen My Children • History Lives • Cooking Up
  History • Rub Against History • Our Heroes! • Learning
  How to Learn • All About Our Town • In the Right
  Direction • What's News? • History on the Go

5. History as Time   **39**
  • Chronology • Empathy • Context • School Days • Put
  Time in a Bottle • Quill Pens and Berry Ink • Time
  Marches On • The Past Anew • Weave a Web • Time to
  Celebrate • It's in the Cards

6. Working with Teachers and Schools   **59**

Resources   **65**

INTRODUCTION

Children are born into history. They have no memory of it, yet they find themselves in the middle of a story that began before they became one of its characters. Children also want to have a place in history — their first historical questions are: "Where did I come from?" and "Was I always here?" These two questions contain the two main meanings of history: It's the story of people and events, and it's the record of times past. And because it's to us that they address these questions, we are in the best position to help prepare our children to achieve the lifelong task of finding their place in history by helping them learn what shaped the world into which they were born. Without information about their history, children don't "get" a lot of what they hear and see around them.

Although parents can be a positive force in helping their children to develop an interest in history, they also can undermine their children's attitudes by saying things such as: "History is boring," or "I hated history class when I was in school." Although you can't make your child like history, you can encourage him/her to do so, and you can take steps to ensure that he/she learns to appreciate its value.

To begin, you can develop some of the following "history habits" that show your child that history is important not only as a school subject but in everyday life.

History Habits

Habits are activities that we do on a regular basis. We acquire habits by choosing to make them a part of our life. It's worth the time and effort to develop good habits because they enhance our well-being. The following history habits can enrich your life experiences and those of your child.

Share family history with your child, particularly your own memories of the people and places of your childhood. Encourage your parents and other relatives to talk with your child about family history.

Read with your child about people and events that have made a difference in the world and discuss the readings together.

Help your child to know that the people who make history are real people just like him/her, and that they have ideas and dreams, work hard and experience failure and success. Introduce your child to local community leaders in person if possible and to national and world leaders (both current and those of the past) by means of newspapers, books, TV and the Internet.

Watch TV programs about important historical topics with your family and encourage discussion about the program as you watch. Check out library books on the same topic and learn more about it. See if the books and TV programs agree on significant issues and discuss any differences.

Make globes, maps and encyclopedias (both print and online versions) available to your child and find ways to use them often. You can use a reference to Asia in your child's favorite story as an opportunity to point out the continent on a globe. You can use the saffron, white and green stripes on a box of spaghetti to help him/her find India on a map and to learn more about its culture by looking it up in the encyclopedia.

Check out from your library or buy a collection of great speeches and other written documents to read with your child from time to time. As you read, pause frequently and try to restate the key points in these documents in language that your child can understand.

Enjoying History with Your Child

As a parent, you can help your child to learn in a way no one else can. That desire to learn is a key to your child's success, and, of course, enjoyment is an important motivator for learning. As you choose activities to do with your child, remember that helping her to learn history doesn't mean that you can't have a good time. In fact, you can teach your child a lot through play. Here are some things to do to make history both fun and productive for you and your child:

1. Use conversation to give your child confidence to learn.

Encouraging your child to talk with you about a topic, no matter how off the mark he/she may seem, lets him/her know that you take his/her ideas seriously and value his/her efforts to learn. The ability to have conversations with your child profoundly affects what and how he/she learns.

2. Let your child know it's OK to ask you questions.

If you can't answer all of his/her questions, that's all right — no one has all the answers. Some of the best answers you can give are, "Good question. How can we find the answer?" and "Let's find out together." Together, you and your child can propose possible answers and then check them by using reference books and the Internet, or by asking someone who is likely to know the correct answers.

3. Make the most of everyday opportunities.

Take advantage of visits from grandparents to encourage storytelling about their lives — What was school like for

them? What was happening in the country and the world? What games or songs did they like? What were the fads of the day? Who are their heroes? On holidays, talk with your child about why the holiday is observed, who (or what) it honors and how and whether it's observed in places other than India. At ball games, talk about the flag and the national anthem and what they mean to the country.

4. Recognize that children have their own ideas and interests.

By letting your child choose some activities that he/she wants to do, you let him/her know that his/her ideas and interests have value. You can further reinforce this interest by asking your child to teach you what he/she learns.

How to Use this Book?

The major portion of this book is made up of activities that you can use with your child to strengthen his/her history knowledge and build strong positive attitudes towards history. And you don't have to be a historian or have a college degree to do them. Your time and interest and the pleasure that you share with your child as part of working together are what matter most. What's far more important than being able to give your child a detailed explanation for the concepts underlying each activity is having the willingness to do the activity with him/her — to read, to ask questions, to search — and to make the learning enjoyable.

In addition to activities, the book also includes:

- Some information about the basics of history;

- Practical suggestions for how to work with teachers and schools to help your child succeed in school; and

A list of resources, such as helpful Web sites and lists of books for you and for your child.

SOME BASICS

What is History?

"Once upon a time..." That opening for many favorite children's tales captures the two main meanings of history — it's the story of people and events, and it's the record of times past. To better understand what history is, let's look closer at each of these two meanings.

The Story in History

Unlike studying science, we study history without being able to directly observe events — they simply are no longer in our presence. "Doing" history is a way of bringing the past to life, in the best tradition of the storyteller. We do this by weaving together various pieces of information to create a story that gives shape to an event.

There are many possible stories about the same event, and there are good storytellers and less good storytellers. Very rarely does one story say it all or any one storyteller "get it right." A good student of history, therefore, tries to determine the true story by looking to see if a storyteller has backed up his/her story with solid evidence and facts.

The history with which we are most familiar is political history — the story of war and peace, important leaders and changes of government. But history is more than that. Anything that has a past has a history, including ideas, such as the idea of freedom, and cultural activities, such as music, art or architecture.

Time in History

Time in history is a kind of relationship. We can look at several events that all happened at the same time and that together tell a story about a particular part of the past. Or we can look at the development of an idea over time and learn how and why it changed. We can consider the relationship between the past and the present, or the future and the past (which is today!). The present is the result of choices that people made and the beliefs they held in the past.

As they prepare to study history, children first need basic knowledge about time and its relationship to change. They need to learn the measures of time, such as year, decade, generation and century. And they need to learn and think about sequences of events as they occurred in time. They need to be able to ask, "About when did that happen?" and to know how to find the answer.

The main focus of history is the relationship between continuity and change. It's important, therefore, that our children understand the difference between them. For example, the population of the India has changed greatly over time with each wave of immigration. As new groups of immigrants entered Indian society, they brought along ideas, beliefs and traditions from their native lands. These new cultures and traditions were woven into existing Indian culture, contributing to its pattern of diversity and making our democratic system of government even stronger. That system continues to evolve to better realize its original purpose of safeguarding our basic human rights of freedom and equal opportunity

A New Look at the Study of History

Studying history is more than memorizing names and dates. Although it's important for citizens to know about great people and events, the enjoyment of history is often found in a "story well told." Here are some suggestions to make the study of history more enjoyable:

·**Original sources make history come alive.** Reading the actual words that changed the course of history and stories that focus on the details of time and place helps children know that history is about real people in real places who made real choices that had some real consequences, and that these people could have made different choices.

Less can mean more. An old proverb tells us that, "A well-formed mind is better than a well-stuffed mind." Trying to learn the entire history of the world is not only impossible, it discourages children and reduces their enthusiasm for history. In-depth study of a few important events gives them a chance to understand the many sides of a story. They can always add new facts.

History is hands-on work. Learning history is best done in the same way that we learn to use a new language, or to play cricket: we do it as well as read about it.

"Doing history" means asking questions about events, people and places; searching our towns for signs of its history; talking with others about current events and issues; and writing our own stories about the past.

Children do well to ask "So what?" Much that we take for granted is not so obvious to children. We need to clarify for them the reasons we ask them to remember certain things. They need to know why it's important to get the facts right. Encouraging children to ask, "So what?" can help them understand what's worth knowing — and why — and so help build critical thinking skills. Being able to think critically prepares children to:

- judge the value of historical evidence;
- judge claims about what is true or good;

- be curious enough to look further into an event or topic;

- be skeptical enough to look for more than one account of an event or life; and

- be aware that how we look at and think about things are often shaped by our own biases and opinions.

Geography: An Important Tool for Learning and Understanding History

Geography affects history — just look at the dramatic changes in world geography over recent years. Governments change, and new countries are born. Many countries no longer have the same names they did even five years ago. Climate changes bring about events such as droughts and floods that cause massive loss of life and migrations of people from one place to another in search of safety. Environmental changes can change the entire history of a community or region.

As with history, children have a natural interest in geography. Watch a group of children playing in the sand. One child makes streets for his cars, while a second child builds houses along the street. A third scoops out a hole and uses the dirt to make a hill, then pours water in the hole to make a lake, using sticks for bridges. The children name the streets, and they may even use a watering can to make rain that washes away a house. They may not realize it, but these children are learning some core features of geography — how people interact with the Earth, how climate affects land, and how places relate to each other through the movement of things from one place to another. When we turn to maps or globes as we talk with our children about vacation plans, events happening around the world or historical events, we teach them a great deal about geography. Not only can such activities help our children learn how to use key reference tools, but over time, they help them from their own mental maps of the world, which allows children to better organize and understand information about other people, places, times and events.

ACTIVITIES

T he activities in this section are arranged into two groups that reflect the meanings of history as story and time. Each group is preceded by a review of three elements of story and time from the perspective of history. The review is meant to give you information that can support your conversations with your child as you do the activities.

For each activity, you'll see a grade span — from pre-school through grade 5 that suggests when children might be ready to try it. Of course, children don't always become interested in or learn the same things at the same time. And they don't suddenly stop enjoying one thing and start enjoying another just because they are a little older. You're the best judge of which activity your child is ready to try. For example, you may find that an activity listed for children in grades 1 or 2 works well with your pre-schooler. On the other hand, you might discover that the same activity may not interest your child until he/she is in grade 3 or 4.

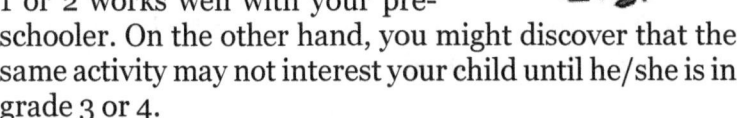

In a highlighted text at the end of each activity, you'll find questions to ask your child about some part of the activity. These questions help your child to develop the critical thinking skills he/she'll need to participate well in society, learn history and learn from history.

When you choose or begin an activity, keep in mind that the reason for doing it is to help your child to learn something about history. Whatever the specific purpose of the activity, make sure that it's clear to your child. The information in the introduction and the questions for each activity can help you to do this. After you complete each activity, discuss with your child what they learned. For example, making bread is one thing, recognizing bread's historical meaning is another. An added bonus: achieving a goal you set together at the beginning of an activity gives your child the pleasure of a completed project.

The materials you need for these activities are found around most homes. Before starting the activities, give your child a notebook — a history log — in which he/she can record his/her own ideas and opinions about each activity. If your child can't yet write, encourage him/her to draw pictures of what he/she sees, or tell you what to write for him/her. In addition, you may want to keep a camera nearby so that your child can include photographs in his/her history log. You may also wish to have him/her decorate and label a shoebox to use for keeping history-related items and project materials.

Finally, feel free to make changes in any activity — shorten or lengthen it — to suit your child's interests and attention span.

We hope that you and your child enjoy the activities and that they inspire you to think of additional activities of your own. Let's get started!

HISTORY AS STORY

The essential elements of history as story are records, narration and evidence.

Records: History is a permanent written record of the past. In more recent times, history is also recorded on film, video, audiotape and through digital technology. You might tell your child that the time before we had any way to record events is called pre-history. It was in pre-historical times that dinosaurs walked the Earth. He/she should also know that before written languages were invented, humans told stories as a way to preserve their identity and important events in their lives. Over time, however, the stories changed as details were forgotten or altered to fit a new situation. Written languages allowed people to keep more accurate records of who they were and what they did so this information could be passed down from generation to generation.

Narration: Narration is storytelling, a way that people interpret events. History, with its facts and evidence, is also an interpretation of the past. A great leader, in his Farewell Address, said: "Though in reviewing the incidents of my administration I am unconscious of intentional error, I am nevertheless too sensible of my defects not to think it probable that I may have committed many errors." Your child needs to be aware that events can have more than one cause and can produce more than one effect, or outcome, and that there is more than one way to look at the relationship between cause and effect.

Evidence: All good histories are based on evidence. Your child needs to learn the importance of evidence, and he/she needs the critical thinking skills to evaluate historical accounts and to determine whether they are based on solid evidence or rely too heavily on personal interpretation and opinion.

Listen My Children

Pre-school - Grade 1

A great way for young children to develop an interest in history is for

parents to make books with history themes a part of their reading-aloud routines.

What You Need?

Picture and read-aloud books about historical people, places and events or with historical settings. For possible titles, see the list of books under the Books for Children heading of the Resources section at the end of this book.

What to Do?

- Talk with your child about the book you're going to read to him/her. Have him/her look at the pictures and notice costumes, types of transportation, houses and other things that show that the book isn't about modern times. Talk with him/her about history — the story of past times.

  - As you read, stop occasionally and ask your child to talk about a character or what is happening in the book. Encourage him/her to ask you questions if he/she doesn't understand something. Explain words he/she may not know and point to objects that he/she may not recognize and tell him/her what they are.

  - Show enthusiasm about reading. Read the book with expression. Make it more interesting by talking as the characters would talk, making sound effects and using facial expressions and gestures.

- Help your child to develop a "library habit." Begin making weekly trips to the library when he/she is very young. See that he/she gets his/her own library card as soon as possible. Many libraries issue cards to children as soon as they can print their names (you'll also have to sign for your child). Regularly choose books with history themes to check out and read at home with him/her. And, when he/she is old enough, encourage him/her to continue this habit.

- After reading a book with a historical theme, encourage your child to make up a play for the family based on the book. If possible, allow him/her to wear a costume or use props that are mentioned in the story.

As you read a book to your child, stop occasionally to ask questions such as the following:
- How do you know this character lived long ago?
- How is this school different from our schools today?
- Do you know what game these children are playing?
- Why did the boy decide to join the Army?
- Can boys that young join the Army today?

What's the Story?

Pre-school - Grade 5

Good history is a story well told. Through storytelling, children are introduced to what's involved in writing the stories that make history. They begin to understand that different people may tell the same story in different ways.

What You Need?

- Family members and friends
- A book of fairy tales or folk tales

What to Do?

- Gather your child and other family members in a

circle and have a storytelling session. Choose a person that you all know well — a relative, friend or neighbor. Begin a group story about that person, explaining that nobody can interrupt the story. Say, for example, "Remember the time that Uncle Mohan decided to help us by fixing that leaky tap in our kitchen?" Then go clockwise around and have each person add to the story. Set a time limit, say three times around the circle so that you must end the story somewhere. Talk about the story. Are there any disagreements about what really happened and what was just opinion — or just added on for fun? If so, how can you settle any differences of opinion about what "really happened"?

- Read aloud a fairy tale or folk tale. You might choose, for example, Beware of Mean Friends or Old Tiger and Greedy Traveler (for more titles, check the Resources section at the end of this book). Talk with your child about how the story begins and ends, who the characters are and what they feel and what happens in the story. Ask him/her how a "made-up" story is different from the story you told about the real person you know.

- Pick a moment in history, for example the fall of the atom bombs on Japan, the storming of the East

India Company in India, the assassination of
Mahatma Gandhi or a current event in the news.
Take your child to your local library and ask the
children's librarian to help you choose books and
other materials about the event that are age-
appropriate for your child. Read the book aloud with
a young child; for an older child, have him/her read
it aloud to you or read it on his/her own and then
talk with him/her about the book.

> **Ask your child:**
> * If you were a TV reporter when the event
>   you read about happened, what would you
>   tell your audience about it?
> * What else would you include?
> * Where would you get your information?
> * How would you check its accuracy?

History Lives

Pre-school - Grade 5

At living history museums children can see people doing
the work of blacksmiths, tin workers, shoemakers, weavers
and others. They can see how things used to be made and
learn how work and daily life have changed over time.

What You Need?

* Visitor brochures and museum maps
* Sketch pad and pencils, or camera

What to Do?

* Plan a visit to a living history museum with your
  child. Write or call the museum ahead of time to
  obtain information brochures and a map. Well-
  known living history museums are located in
  metropolitan cities, but smaller museums can be

found in many other places across the country. If you can't visit a museum, travel there by reading books or conducting "virtual" tours on the Internet.

- Talk with your child about the information in the brochures and what he/she can expect to see at the museum. Make sure that he/she understands that what he/she will see is life the way it was once actually lived — not make-believe.

- Help your child to sketch something in the museum and put it in his/her history log. Apprise him/her that drawings were the only way events available for keeping records before introduction of camera.

- Use your camera to make a modern record of history and create a scrapbook with the photographs of what you saw.

- When you reach home, ask your child what his/her favorite object or activity is and why. Talk with your child about what it would have been like to live in that historical place in that period of time. Your family might pretend to be living in the historical place. Try spending an evening "long ago," without using electrical lights and other appliances such as TVs and microwave ovens. How is life without those luxuries different from your life today?

Ask your child:
- How were days spent in the period of time you experienced?
- What kind of dress was common, or special?
- What kinds of food did people usually eat, and did they eat alone or in groups? What kind of work would you have chosen to do as an adult?
- If a living history museum were made of life today, what would people of the future see and learn there?

Cooking Up History

Kindergarten - Grade 5

Every culture has its version of bread. Children enjoy making this native Indian fry bread. (Check the Bibliography and Resources sections of this book for books that contain other recipes from history).

What You Need?

- 2 1/2 cups all-purpose or wheat flour
- 1 1/2 tablespoons baking powder
- 1 teaspoon salt
- 1 tablespoon dried skimmed milk powder
- 3/4 cup warm water
- 1 tablespoon vegetable oil
- Oil for frying
- Mixing bowls and spoons, spatula
- Large frying pan
- Cloth towels
- Baking sheet
- Paper towels

What to Do?

- Talk with your child about native Indian peoples — that they lived in what is now the India for thousands of years before non-native peoples came here, and that many tribes still live throughout India.

- Read a book with your child about native Indian life, both long ago and today, either fiction or non-fiction. With an older child, search the Internet for native tribes, such as Bodo, Gond and Khasis. Explore Web sites to learn about tribes' geographic locations, tribal activities and programs.

- Have your child help you gather all of the ingredients listed above. For a younger child, talk about what you're doing as you complete each step in the recipe.

Your older child can complete the steps as you read them aloud. **Reminder:** You'll need to supervise your child closely, regardless of his age, as you work around a hot stove! Follow this recipe:

-   In a large bowl, stir together the flour, baking powder and salt. In a small bowl, stir together the dried milk, water and vegetable oil. Pour this liquid over the dry ingredients and stir until the dough is smooth (1 or 2 minutes). Add 1 tablespoon of flour if the dough is too soft.

-   Knead the dough in the bowl with your hands about 30 seconds. Cover it with a cloth and let it sit 10 minutes.

-   Line the baking sheet with paper towels to receive the finished loaves.

-   Divide the dough into eight sections. Take one section and keep the rest covered in the bowl. Roll the dough into a ball and flatten with your hand. Then roll it into a very thin circle 8 to 10 inches across. The thinner the dough, the puffier the bread will be. Cover this circle with a cloth. Continue with the other seven sections of dough in the same way.

-   In the large frying pan, pour vegetable oil to about 1 inch deep. As you begin to roll the last piece of dough, turn on the heat under the frying pan. When the oil is hot, slip in a circle of dough. Fry for about 1 minute or until the bottom is golden brown. Turn the dough over with tongs or a spatula. Fry the other side for 1 minute.

-   Put the fry bread on the baking sheet and continue with the other rounds of dough.

-   Eat your fry bread while it's hot and crisp. Put honey on it if you like.

- Help your child to use the Internet or reference books to find out more about the role of bread in human history.

Ask your child:
  - How is this bread different from the breads you usually eat?
  - What place does bread have in our daily lives and in the lives of people in other cultures?

Rub against History

Grades 1-3

Younger children find making rubbings great fun. Cornerstones and plaques are interesting, and even coins will do.

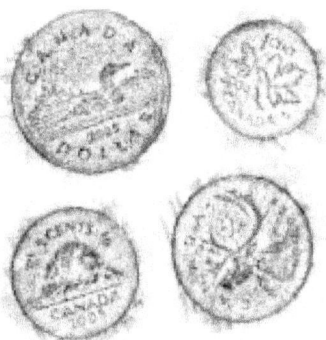

What You Need?

- Tracing paper or other lightweight paper
- Large crayons with the paper removed, fat lead pencil, colored pencils, or artists' charcoal
- Coins

What to Do?

- Use the list above to help your child make a kit to do rubbings. Choose paper that does not tear easily, but also is light enough so that the details of the rubbing will be visible.

- Begin by having your child make a rubbing of a one rupee coin or five rupee coin (large coins from other countries or commemorative coins can be interesting to use, too). Tape the coin to a surface to make it stable. Double the tape so that it sticks on both sides and place it on the bottom of the coin. Attach the coin to a piece of wood or to some surface that can't be harmed by the tape. Lay the paper on top of the coin, and have your child rub across it with a pencil, crayon or charcoal. Tell him/her not to rub too hard and to keep rubbing until the coin's marks show up on the paper. Talk with him/her about what the rubbing shows.

- Take your child on a walk around the neighborhood. Look for objects that he/she can use for rubbings, such as dates in the sidewalk, words on cornerstones and plaques on buildings or interesting designs on bricks or other materials used on buildings. Once home, ask family members to view the rubbings and guess what each represents. Ask your child to tell the story behind the rubbings and why he/she chose to make them.

- Consider taking your older child to cemeteries or memorial sites around town and make rubbings of old gravestones or markers. Talk with him/her about each rubbing. Tell him/her to look for designs and dates and ask him/her questions to make sure that he/she knows how old the objects are.

- Encourage your child to cut out some of his/her rubbings and include them in his/her history log.

Ask your child:
- What showed up in your rubbings?
- What did the date and designs commemorate?
- Historical preservation groups in India have worked to preserve old buildings and to install plaques on public historical places.
- Do you think that this is important work?
- Why have humans left their marks on the world from early cave drawings to today's monuments, such as the India Gate?
- If you made a monument, what would it be?
- Who or what would it help people to remember or honor?

Our Heroes!

Grades 3-5

Heroes are everywhere. Sharing stories about them with children can help them understand that heroes come from many different walks of life and that their courageous acts occur in many different places and times.

What You Need?

Family photographs; newspaper and pictures from books or the Internet of both local and national figures who have been recognized for community service, bravery or selfless acts.

What to Do?

- Select a photo of someone in your family who has an admirable quality or who performed a courageous act. You might choose a grandparent who left everything behind to immigrate to India or your mother who sacrificed so that you could have a good education or your father who fought in a war or your brother who took a stand on a controversial issue. Sit with your child and tell him/her about the relative's life. Talk with him/her about the qualities of heroism that the relative showed — courage, self-discipline, responsibility, citizenship and so forth.

• Show your child newspaper pictures of local people who have performed acts of courage or service to the community. Talk with him/her about what the people did and why they are considered heroes. In addition to individuals, choose groups of people who have been called heroes, such as firefighters and policemen.

• Show your child pictures of historical figures who have been called heroes. Choose people whom you admire and feel comfortable talking about with your child. Choose groups as well, such as the revolutionaries who opposed slavery before the Independence or the people who participated in the freedom struggle movement.

Ask your child:
- What does it mean to be a hero? Is it easy and fun to be a hero?
- What qualities do heroes seem to have? Who are your heroes? Why?
- What would you like to tell one of your heroes?

Learning How to Learn

Grades 3-5

Local newspapers, phone books and other handy resources can serve as guides to local history. Teaching children how to use them gives them a great tool for finding many sources of information.

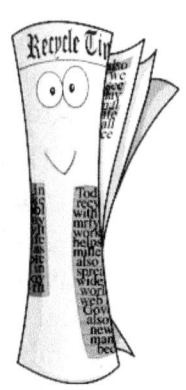

What You Need?

- Phone books, both yellow and white pages Local newspapers

What to Do?

- Help your child make a list of his/her interests. Include the sports, hobbies, history topics, animals and music he/she likes.

- With your child, look through your local newspapers for lists of things to do in the community. Look for parades, museum and art exhibits, music events, children's theater, history talks, guided walks through historical places or tours of historical homes. Choose an event in which you can both participate.

- Sit with your child and show him/her how to use the phone book to find information. For example, in the yellow pages, look for the heading "Museums." Talk with your child about the places that you find listed there — What different kinds of museums are listed? Are they nearby? Look especially for history museums.

  - Brainstorm with your child about what other headings you might look under to find information about local history. Try, for example, "Historical Societies." (If your phone book has a special section of information about community services and points of interest, look there as well).

  - Call the historical museums and societies that you find. Ask about their programs for children, their hours and upcoming special events. Also ask where else you should go to learn about your town's history.

  - Have your child listen to your phone conversation and model for him/her how to ask for information.

- Have your child begin a list in his/her history log of local historical sites. Tell him/her to include phone numbers, addresses, hours of operation and other useful information for future visits.

Ask your child:
  - If you were asked to be a tour guide for visitors to our town, what would you show them?
  - If you went to another town, how would you go about finding out about its past?

All About Our Town

Grades 3-5

A good place for children to begin to develop an interest in history is to find out the history of where they live.

What You Need?

Guides and histories of your town or city

What to Do?

- With your child, research the history of the town, city or area in which you live. Begin by asking your child what he/she already knows, then ask him/her to make some predictions about what you will find out regarding when your area was first settled, who the first settlers were, where they came from, and why they chose to settle in the area. Help him/her to record these predictions in his/her history log.

  - Go with your child to the local library, or sit with him/her at a computer, and look for historical reference materials — local histories and guidebooks, articles in regional historical magazines, and so forth (your librarian can direct you to good sources of information). As you work, talk with your child about what you're finding.

  - Afterwards, talk with your child about what you found out.

- As part of this activity, focus your child's attention on your area's geography as it played a part in its history. Was it settled because it's on a waterway? Did it grow into a large town because of its location? its climate? Did industry develop there because coal, oil or copper deposits were nearby?

Ask your child:
- What is the most surprising thing you learned about our town's history?
- What's the most interesting old building that you found?
- Were there any historical markers or monuments that you discovered in our town?
- Who is your favorite person to talk to for stories about our town's past?

In the Right Direction

Grades 3-5

In order to talk and learn about places, and to locate themselves and others in terms of place, children need to understand and be able to name geographic directions.

What You Need?

- Maps of your state, a globe or an atlas
- Blank paper and crayons or colored pencils

What to Do?

- Sit with your younger child at a table or on the floor so that you can both see a map of your state. Point out where you live, explain the directional signs on the map: north, south, east and west. Mention several nearby towns or cities that your child has visited or knows about. Point to one of these and say, for example, "Grandfather lives here, in Mumbai. That's north of our town." Have your child use her finger to trace the line from your location to that place. Continue by pointing out places that are south, east and west of your location. When your child catches on to directions, ask him/her to point to places that are north, south, east and west of where he/she lives.

- For your older child, make the map activity into a game. When you have made sure that he/she understands directions, pick a place on the map and give clues about its location, for example, "I'm looking at a city that is west of Lucknow and east of Jaipur." (You can also name rivers, lakes, mountains or other geographic features that can be seen on the map). When your child gets the right answer, have him/her choose a place and give directional clues for you to use to find it.

- As part of your child's study of national and world history, help him/her to use an atlas or globe to locate places mentioned in his/her textbook.

- Help to make directional words a part of your child's vocabulary by using them yourself in daily conversation. Rather than saying, "We're turning right at the next corner," say, "We're turning east at the next corner." Encourage him/her to use the words as well.

- Give your child blank paper and crayons or colored pencils and ask him/her to draw a map of your neighborhood showing important buildings and landmarks (religious places, schools, malls, statues, rivers, hills and so on). Remind him/her to include an indicator of direction on the map. After he/she's finished, talk with him/her about what the map shows and have him/her give specific descriptions about the locations of various places on it.

Ask your child:
- Why is it important to be able to read a map or use a globe?
- How can knowing something about locations help you in studying history?

What's News?

Grades 3-5

What's new today really began in the past. Discussing the news is a way to help children gain a historical perspective on the events of the present.

What You Need?

- Newspapers
- Weekly news magazine
- A daily national TV news program
- Atlas or globe
- Highlighter

What to Do?

This activity can be most useful to younger children if it's done from time to time to get them used to the idea of "news." Older children benefit from doing it more often, at least once a week if possible.

- Look through the daily newspaper or a recent news magazine with your child. Ask him/her to decide what pictures or headlines have some connection to history. For example, a news story about the signing of a peace treaty might also show pictures of similar events, such as the signing of the Shimla agreement, from the past. A story about the current Indian leader might give a historical overview and show pictures of Mahatma Gandhi, Annie Besant and C.V. Raman. A story on a Supreme Court ruling that affects school integration might have a headline that mentions in the Right of Children to Free and Compulsory Education Act, 2009. Use a highlighter to mark these references.

  - With your child, read the articles you've chosen. Make a list (or have him/her do it) of any references to events that did not happen today or yesterday, or to people who died some time ago.

  - Talk with your child about what these past events and people have to do with events happening today. Help him/her record these connections in his/her history log.

- Watch the evening news or a morning news program with your child. Help him/her to write as many references as possible to past history. Discuss the links he/she finds between these references and the news story you heard. In an atlas or on a globe, help him/her point out where the stories he/she watched took place.

- During another session of TV viewing, help your child focus on how the information was communicated: did the newscaster use interviews, books, historical records, written historical accounts, literature, paintings, photographs? Did the newscaster report "facts"? Did he/she express opinions?

- Help your child compare several accounts of a major news story from different news shows, newspapers and news magazines.

Ask your child:
- Did you find anything "new" in the news?
- What "same old stories" did you find?
- What's the difference between "fact" and "opinion"?

History on the Go

Grades 3-5

Visiting the historical places that children read about in their history books reinforces for them that history is about real people, places and events.

What You Need?

- Your child's history book
- Maps, guidebooks

What to Do?

- Find out what historical events your child is studying in school. Then check to see if a place related to those events is nearby and arrange to visit it with your child. If such a place isn't nearby, arrange for a "virtual" visit by looking for age-appropriate Web sites.

  - Whether your visit is real or virtual, work with your child to prepare for it together. You might, for example, ask your local librarian to help you and your child find books, DVDs and videotapes about the history of the place you plan to visit or about the historical figures who lived there.

  - Call the visitor information centers for the area and request to send maps and specially prepared guidebooks (you can usually find such centers through Internet searches or by consulting travel books in your local library).

  - Study maps or the area with your child. Talk with him/her about the best way to get from your home to the site. As you travel, have him/her follow the route on the map.

  - Help your child make a list of questions to ask on your trip.

  - Talk with him/her about the place you're visiting.

  - After the visit, have your child make up a quiz for you, or a game, that is based on what he/she learned during the trip.

  - Encourage your child to read more about the place you visited and the people who were part of its history. Especially encourage your older child to find historical documents that are associated with the site. For example, if you visit

the site of the National Commission for
Protection of Child Rights, which is in New Delhi,
you might have him/her read — or read to him/
her — section of Activities"

Ask your child to identify any geographical features of
the site you visited that played a part in the historical event
he/she studied. If, for example, you visit a Jallianwala Bagh,
you might point out its significance that how British Indian
Army soldiers under the command of Brigadier-General
Reginald Dyer opened fire on an unarmed gathering of men,
women and children on April 13, 1919.

Ask your child:
- What was historical about the place you visited?
- What kinds of things communicated the history of the place?
- Did the visit make you see our town in a new way?
- Even though the place we visited was not in our town, did it make you think of something historical from where we live?

HISTORY AS TIME

The essential elements of history as time are chronology, empathy and context.

Chronology

Although our children need the opportunity to study historical events in depth to get an understanding of them, they also need to know the time *sequence* of those events as well as the names of the people and places associated with them. When we are able to locate events in time, we are better able to learn the *relationships* among them. What came first? What was cause, and what was effect? Without a sense of chronological order, events seem like a big jumble, and we can't understand what happened in the past. It's important that children be able to identify causes of events such as economic depressions and to understand the effects of those events. These are skills that are crucial to critical thinking and to being productive and informed citizens.

Empathy

Empathy is the ability to imagine ourselves in the place of other people and times. To accurately imagine ourselves in the place of people who lived long ago, we must have an idea of what it was like "to be there." This requires learning about both the world in which a person lived and that person's reactions to the world. For example, in studying the westward expansion across our country, children need to be aware of how very difficult travel was in that time. They may ask why people didn't just take airplanes to avoid the dangers they faced on the wagon trails. When parents explain that people then couldn't fly because airplanes hadn't yet been invented, children may ask why not. They need an understanding of how technology develops and of the technology that was available at the time of a historical event. Just knowing the physical surroundings of a person at a point in time, however, doesn't allow children to develop empathy. Stories and documents that tell us about people's feelings and reactions to events in their lives allow us to recognize the human feelings we share with people across space and time. Helping children find and use original source documents from the past, such as diaries, journals and speeches, gives them a way to learn to see events through the eyes of people who were there.

Context

Context is related to empathy. Context means "weave together," and refers to the set of circumstances in several areas that surround an event. To understand any historical period or event children should know *how to weave* together **politics** (how a society was governed), **sociology** (what groups of people formed the society), **economics** (how people worked and what they produced), **place** (where the events happened) and **religion**, **literature**, the **arts** and **philosophy** (what people valued and believed at the time). When children try to understand the Indian freedom movement, for example, they will uncover a complex set of events. And they will find that these events draw their meaning from their context.

History means having a grand old time with new stories. So, as you and your child do the following activities, help him/her to think about the relationship between history and time.

School Days

Kindergarten - Grade 3

A good way to introduce children to history is to let them know how school — a main focus of their lives — has changed over the years.

What You Need?

- Map of India
- Crayons or colored pencils

What to Do?

- Talk with your child about what school was like when you were a child. Include how schools looked physically; the equipment teachers used; what subjects you studied; what choices you faced; and your favorite teachers and activities. If possible, show family photographs of yourself or other family members participating in school activities — playing a sport, cheerleading, giving a speech, winning an award, talking with classmates, working in a science lab and so forth. Have your child notice such things as clothing and hair styles, the way the school building or classroom looked, the equipment being used. Have him/her compare the school's characteristics with that of his/her own.

- Join your child in exploring what school was like 50 or 100 years ago. Ask your librarian for help in looking this up, talk to older relatives and neighbors and use the Internet. Again, include photographs when possible.

  - With your older child talk about some of the history of work in India and explain how it affects schooling. Tell him/her, for example, that many years ago, when India was a largely agricultural society, children were needed at home to help plant and harvest crops. Because of this, children often didn't go to school everyday, or at all in the summer. In addition, the school year was more or less matched to the time of year that was less busy on farms — the late fall and winter months.

- Next explain that when India was switching from an agricultural to a manufacturing society, some children worked long days in factories, doing hard, dangerous jobs. Eventually, laws were passed to keep factories from using children to do dangerous work. Along with these child labor laws, other laws were passed that officially required children to go to school until a certain age.

• Ask your child to imagine what school will you like in the future. Your younger child may want to use blocks to build a future schoolhouse, and your older child may want to draw or write about theirs.

Ask your child:

• What has remained the same about school from the past to the present?
• What has changed?
• If you could be the head of a school 20 years from now, what would you keep and what would you change based on your current school?
• How would you go about making these changes?

Put Time in a Bottle

Kindergarten - Grade 3

Collecting things from their lifetimes and putting them in a time capsule is a history lesson that children will never forget.

What You Need?

• Magazines or newspapers
• Sealable container

- Camera
- Tape or other sealant

What to Do?

- Talk with your child about time capsules. Explain that when buildings such as schools, courthouses and temples are built, people often include a time capsule — a special container into which they place items that can tell about their lives and times to future generations who open the container.

  - Tell your child that you want to help him/her make his/her own personal time capsule. Talk with him/her about what he/she might want to put in it.

  - Have him/her use a simple camera to take pictures of a few important objects in his/her life — a favorite CD, poster or pair of shoes; a baseball bat, football jersey or cricket; his/her computer, music player or cell phone. Have him/her locate and add magazine pictures of games and toys; cars, airplanes and other types of transportation; different kinds of sporting events; and clothes. Next have him/her locate examples of slang, ads for movies and TV shows, and selections from important speeches, poetry and stories or novels. Also help him/her find stories about current heroes and local, national and world events; and accounts of current issues and crises. Finally have him/her write a letter to someone in the future that describes life today.

- Call the family together and have your child do a "show and tell" of the items he/she's collected.

- Once everyone is satisfied with the collection, help your child to label the items with his/her name and with any other information that will help those who find them understand how they are significant to the history of our time.

- Have him/her place the items in a container, seal the container and find a place to store it.

- Have him/her write in his/her history log a short description of what he/she has done and record the date. Encourage him/her to draw a map that shows the location of the time capsule and to use the correct directional words to label it.

• Try to find news stories (your local newspaper, library or local historical society or museum can often direct you to such stories) about the opening of such a capsule in your area and what was in it. If possible, take your child to look at the contents of an opened time capsule — perhaps at your local historical society or museum. Also try to locate buildings in your area that contain unopened time capsules. Take your child to see the buildings and point out the cornerstones — the places in which most capsules are placed. Talk with him/her about the information on the cornerstone.

Ask your child:

  • What did the collection of items tell you about the period in which we live?
  • Did the items tend to be of a certain type?

Quill Pens and Berry Ink

Grades 1-3

History depends on writing, and
writing has changed over time from
scratches on clay to digitalized codes
and letters.

What You Need?

- For quill pen:
    - feather, scissors, a paper clip
- For berry ink:
    - 1/2 cup of ripe berries (blueberries, cherries,
      blackberries, strawberries, or raspberries work
      well), 1/2 teaspoon salt, 1/2 teaspoon vinegar,
      food strainer, bowl, wooden spoon, small jar with
      tight-fitting lid
- Paper
- Paper towels

What to Do?

- Place the berries in the strainer and hold it over the
  bowl. Have your child use the wooden spoon to crush
  the berries against the strainer so that the juice drips
  into the bowl. When all the juice is out of the berries,
  throw the pulp away. Tell your child to add the salt
  and vinegar to the berry juice and stir it well. If the
  ink is too thick, have him/her add a teaspoon or
  two of water (not too much or he/she'll lose the
  color). Help him/her to pour the juice into a small
  jar and close it with a tight-fitting lid. (**Note**: Make
  only as much ink as you will use at one time, because
  it will dry up quickly).
- Have your child watch as you form the pen point by

cutting the fat end of the feather on an angle, curving the cut slightly. (**Note:** A good pair of scissors is safer than a knife. But play it safe, and always do the cutting yourself). Clean out the inside of the quill so that the ink will flow to the point. Use the end of a paper clip if needed. You may want to cut a center slit in the point; however, if you press too hard on the pen when you write, it may split.

- Give the quill pen to your child and tell him/her to dip just the tip in the ink. Keep a paper towel handy to use as an ink blotter. Allow him/her to experiment by drawing lines and curves and by making designs and single letters. Show him/her how to hold the pen at different angles to get different effects.

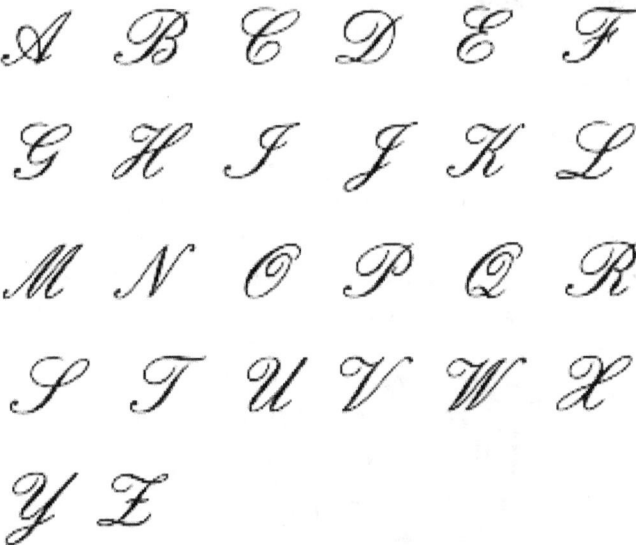

- Have him/her practice signing his/her name, ancient style, with the early English letters shown below. Then have him/her write his signature in his history log.

- Have him/her write his/her name again, using a pen or pencil. Talk with him/her about how the signatures are alike and different.

Ask your child:

- Why do we write?
- When do people in our family use writing?
- What written things do you see every day?
- What are their different purposes?
- What effect do different writing tools have on writing, for example quill pens, ballpoint pens, typewriters and computers?

Time Marches On

Grades 2-5

The stories of history have beginnings, middles and ends that show events and suggest causes and effects. Making personal timelines can help children to understand these elements. They allow children to use events in their own lives to gain a sense of time, to understand the sequence in which things happen and to see connections between causes and effects.

What You Need?

- Large sheet of paper (Kraft paper, for example)
- Yardstick and ruler
- Shelf paper
- Colored pencils or crayons
- Removable tape

What to Do?

- Sit with your younger child at a table. On a piece of paper, draw a vertical line. Explain that this is a time line. Use different colored pencils or crayons to make straight marks on the line in even intervals and label the marks 1, 2, 3, 4, 5, 6, 7 and so forth. Explain to your child that each mark is a year in his/her life.

    - Beneath the first mark, write "I was born." Then point to another mark and ask your child what he/she remembers about that year in his/her life. Help him/her to choose one important event from that year, then think of a label to write. Continue with the remaining years, filling in events for those early years that he/she can't recall.

    - Review the timeline. Allow your child to erase and change an event for a particular year if he/she remembers one that he/she thinks is more important. (Tell him/her that historians also rethink their choices when they study history).

- Have your older child make a timeline *poster* by placing a long piece of shelf paper on the floor. Have her/him use a yardstick to draw a line that is three feet long.

    - Talk with your child about important dates in her/his life — the day he/she was born; his/her first day of kindergarten, of first grade; the day his/her best friend moved in next door; and so forth. Tell him/her to write the dates on the line. Invite him/her to add dates that are important for the whole family — the day his/her baby brother/sister was born, the day his/her favorite uncle got married, the day the family moved to a new place, the day a grandparent died and so on. If appropriate photos are available, have him/her add them to the timeline.

- For a horizontal timeline, use removable tape to fasten the paper to the wall, making sure it's placed at a level that is easy for your child to see and continue working on. For a vertical timeline, hang the paper next to the doorway in your child's room.

- Display the finished timeline and ask your child to tell other family members and friends what it shows.

- Have your child expand his/her timeline by adding events that were happening in the world at the same time as each event of his/her life. Help him/her use the Internet or the library's collection of newspapers to find and record the headlines for each of his/her birthdays.

Ask your child:

- What is the most important event on the timeline?
- What effects did the event have on your life?
- What are the connections between the events in your life and world events?

The Past Anew

Grades 3-5

Re-enactments of historical battles or periods, such as colonial times, make our nation's history come alive — and get children involved.

What You Need?

- A library card
- Local newspapers
- Phone book

What to Do?

- Explain to your child what re-enactments are — people dressing in the costumes and acting out what life was like at some earlier time. With him/her, find out whether and where local re-enactments are held by looking in your local newspaper or calling your local historical society, a state park. If possible, choose a re-enactment to visit. Prepare your child by taking him/her to a local museum or historical site that relates to the re-enactment, by watching a TV program about the event or period or by searching for information about it on the Internet.

- - Attend the re-enactment and participate.
- - Ask — and encourage your child to ask — the re-enactors questions about anything, from why they wear particular kinds of hats to the

meanings of the event or period for the development or transformation of India.

Ask your child:

- What was unusual or interesting about the re-enactment?
- What role did each of the re-enactors play?
- If there was conflict, what was shown or said about its causes and effects?
- What obstacles did the characters face? How did they overcome them?
- What is the difference between the "real thing" and a performance of it?
- What did you learn from the performance?

Weave a Web

Grades 4-5

A history web is a way of connecting people and events.

What You Need?

- Large piece of paper or poster board (at least 3.5 ft. x 2.5 ft.)
- Colored pencils, crayons or markers

What to Do?

- As you walk around your neighborhood with your child, point out interesting buildings, statues or other features. For example, you might pick a place in your community that has always seemed mysterious to you — an old ball field; a store, strange house or courthouse; a church, fountain, monument, clock or school building. Have your child study the place and write in his/her history log what he/she sees and hears. For example, have him/her look for plaques, engravings or other marks on buildings, such as dates and designs, or for unusual features, such as bleachers, windows or bell towers.

- Help him/her to find information about the place by asking a librarian for resources, by searching the archives of the local newspaper, or by using the Internet. Tell him/her to be on the lookout for events that happened there, such as athletic records that might have been set or visits by a famous person. Also have him/her look for things that changed the place, such as the addition or removal of rooms, stairs or parking lots.

• Help your child to locate people who have lived in your town a long time. Arrange for him/her to interview them using questions about the place he/she studied and the events surrounding it, and about any important events in the town's history that they remember.

• Help him/her draw a web. Begin by placing the name of the place he/she studied in the middle (like the spider who weaves a "home"). Then have him/her draw several lines (strands) from the middle to show the major events in the life of the place. To finish, have him/her connect the strands with cross lines to show other related events. When the web is complete, talk with your child about the relationships among the strands.

• Have your child send his/her web to the editor of your local newspaper and ask to have it published. He/she can write about the web and ask readers to contribute more information to add to it. Tell him/her that this is exactly how "real" history is written!

- Newspapers often include timelines of events. Point these out to your child and talk with him/her about what they show.

Ask your child:

- When was the place you picked built?
- How the place you picked is connected to other events in history?

Time to Celebrate

Grades 4-5

On coins and notes is written the phrase "Satyameva Jayate," which is Sanskrit for "Truth Alone Triumphs." It is an appropriate phrase to describe how our country has developed and the many different people and groups who have made it so great.

What You Need?

- Indian coins
- Map of the world
- Calendar

What to Do?

- Have your child look at Indian coins for the phrase "Satyameva Jayate." Explain that the phrase means "Truth Alone Triumphs," and that it refers to our country as one nation with many peoples and cultures. Explain that it isn't our families' ethnic heritages that bind us together as Indians, but shared democratic values.

  With your child, talk about the following holidays that are celebrated in India. Look at a calendar and

add other holidays, if you choose. Next to each
holiday write (or have him/her write) when it's
celebrated and what it celebrates.

New Year's Day	January 1	New beginning
Republic Day	January 26	Came into force the Constitution of India
Holi	On the last full moon day of the lunar month Phalguna (February/March)	Marks the dawn of the spring season
Labor Day	May 1	To celebrate the economic and social achievements of workers
Independence Day	August 15	Adoption of the Declaration of Independence in 1947
Gandhi Jayanti	October 2	Birthday of Mahatma Gandhi
Dussehra	The day after Navratri	The victory of Gods over demons
Diwali	Occurring between mid-October and mid-November	To signify the triumph of good over evil
Eid	On the first day of the month Shawwal	Marks the end of Ramadan, the Islamic holy month of fasting
Christmas Day	December 25	Birth of Christ

- When you are talking about holidays, take the
  opportunity to read original source materials related
  to them. For example: on Children's Day, read one
  of the great prime ministerial speeches such as

Jawaharlal Nehru's *A Tryst With Destiny* or Mahatma Gandhi's "Quit India" speech; Vivekananda at the Chicago World's Parliament of Religions in 1893. Talk with your child about the meaning of each speech.

• Encourage your child to find out about national holidays that are celebrated in other nations. Classmates, neighbors and relatives from other countries are good sources of information.

• Invite your child to think and talk about other important holidays that he/she thinks our nation should celebrate. Are their any people he/she thinks deserve to have a holiday of their own? Any group of people? Any event that needs to be celebrated that isn't?

• Discuss with your child your family's personal celebrations, and have him/her write in his/her history log about these special days.

Ask your child:

• What kinds of accomplishments or events do we celebrate in India?
• What similarities and differences did you find between Indian holidays and holidays celebrated by people from other countries?

It's in the Cards

Grades 4-5

Many children don't like to study history in school because they are asked to memorize so many dates and names.

Parents can help — and make learning more enjoyable — by using games to reinforce what their children are learning in history class.

What You Need?

- Your child's history book
- Index cards or sheets of heavy paper cut into cards

What to Do?

- Find out what events your child is currently studying in school. Use information from his/her textbook to make a set of cards. On one card, write the name of a historical figure; on a second card, write the events for which that figure is known in history; and on a third card, write the date(s) for the event. Do this for four or five figures from the time being studied.

  - Use the cards to review with your child, helping him/her to name each figure and match it with the events and dates.

  - When your child is comfortable with the cards, shuffle them and deal an equal number to your child and to yourself. Choose one of your cards and read it aloud. Say, for example, "Raja Rammohan Roy." If your child has the event (Sati Practice) or date ("1829" — the year he abolished the Sati practice), he/she must give you the card. If he/she has the card, he/she must give it to you, and you continue asking for cards. If he/she doesn't have the card, the turn goes to

him/her, and he/she asks you for a card.
Continue until one of you has no cards left.

- Ask your child to think of other ways to use card
games to learn more about history.

> **Ask your child:**
>
> - Why is it important to know when things happened?
> - Why could some things not have happened any earlier than they did?
> - What would happen to the story of times past if our cards got all mixed up and out of order?

6 WORKING WITH TEACHERS AND SCHOOLS

Research has shown that children at all grade levels do better in school, feel more confident about themselves as learners and have higher expectations for themselves when their parents are supportive of and involved with their education. Here are some ways that you can stay involved in your child's school life and support his learning of history:

Become familiar with your child's school. During your visit, look for clues as to whether the school values history. For example, ask yourself:

- What do I see in my child's school and classroom to show that history is valued? For example, are maps, globes, atlases, and history related student work visible?

- Are newspapers, news magazines and other current events publications part of the history curriculum? Are videos, computer programs and collections of original source materials included in the study of history? Are textbooks and other resources up to date and accurate?

- Does the school library contain a range of history-related materials, including biographies and historical fiction as well as information about local, state, national and world history, culture, societies and geography? If so, are they recent publications?

Find out about the school's history curriculum. Ask for a school handbook. If none is available, meet with the school's principal and ask questions such as the following:

- What methods and materials does the school use for history instruction? Are these methods based on sound research evidence about what works best? Are the materials up to date? Can students do hands on projects? Is the curriculum well coordinated across grades, from elementary school through middle school? Does the curriculum include both world history and Indian history?

- Are the history teachers highly qualified? Do they meet state certification and subject-area knowledge requirements?

- How much instructional time is spent on history?

- How does the school measure student progress in history? What tests does it use? Do the tests assess what students are actually taught in their classes?

- How do the students at the school score on state assessments of history?

- Are activities available that parents can use at home to supplement and support instruction?

- If you feel dissatisfied with the history curriculum, talk to your child's teacher first, and then to the principal, the head of the history curriculum division, the school superintendent and, finally, members of the school board. Also ask other parents for their opinions and suggestions.

- If you have not seen it, ask to look at the report card for your school. These report cards show how your school compares to others in the district and indicate how well it is succeeding.

Meet with your child's teacher. Schedule an appointment and ask how your child approaches history. Does he/she enjoy it? Does he/she participate actively? Does he/she understand assignments and do them accurately? If the teacher indicates that your child has problems, ask for specific things that you can do to help him/her. In addition, you can do the following:

- Attend parent-teacher conferences early in the school year. Listen to what the teacher says during these conferences and take notes.

- Let the teacher know that you expect your child to gain a knowledge of history, and that you appreciate his/her efforts towards this goal.

- Ask the teacher what his/her expectations are for the class and your child.

- Agree on a system of communication with the teacher for the year, either by phone, e-mail or through letters.

- Keep an open mind in discussing your child's education with the teacher; ask questions about anything you don't understand; and be frank with him/her about your concerns.

Compliment the teacher's efforts with your child. Let him/her know how much you appreciate his/her commitment to all the children he/she teaches.

Visit your child's classroom. In the classroom, look for the following:

- Do teachers display a thorough knowledge of their subjects? Do they relay this knowledge to students in ways that students can understand?

- Do students discuss their ideas and offer explanations? Do they have opportunities to talk and work with each other as well as with the teacher? Are they encouraged to ask questions in class? Are they learning how to identify reliable sources of information and how to use them to find answers?

- Does the instruction show students how to connect historical information they're learning to their personal experiences and to explore how past events affect their lives?

- Are students regularly assigned history homework? Do assignments involve history projects, including posters or displays, debates, mock trials and role playing?

- Does the class go on field trips that relate to history?

For example, does the class visit historical sites, history museums, local historians or local elected officials?

- Does the teacher expect — and help — *all* students to succeed? Does he/she encourage them to set high goals for themselves? Does he/she listen to their explanations and ideas?

- Do classroom tests and assessments match national, state and local history standards? Requirement of annual assessments of students according to state-defined standards and the dissemination of the results to parents, teachers, principals and others. Curricula based on state standards should be taught in the classroom; thus assessment would be aligned with instruction. In addition to assessments, are teachers using many different ways to determine if children know and understand history, including asking open-ended questions that require thought and analysis? Do assessments match what has been taught? Are they used appropriately to plan instruction and evaluate student understanding?

Find out if the school has a Web site. School Web sites can provide you with ready access to all kinds of information, including homework assignments, class schedules, lesson plans and dates for school district and state tests.

Get actively involved. Attend meetings of parent-teacher organizations. If you're unable to attend, ask that the minutes of the meetings be sent to you, or that they be made available on the school's Web site. If your schedule permits, volunteer to help with the history program. Teachers often send home lists of ways in which parents can get involved, including the following:

- Assisting with classroom projects;
- Educational trips;

- Offering to set up a history display in the school's front hallway or in your child's classroom;

- Leading hands-on lessons (if you have a good history background yourself);

- Helping in a computer laboratory or other area requiring adult supervision; and

- Starting a drive to raise money for computers, books or field trips.

Even if you can't volunteer for work *at* the school, you can help your child learn when you're at home. The key question is, "What can I do at home, easily and every day, to reinforce and extend what the school is teaching?" This is the involvement that every parent can and must provide.

RESOURCES

Web Sites

The following Web sites are some of the many that contain great links for both you and your child. Most provide you and your child with information about how to search for specific information and with links to other age-appropriate sites.

Indian History:

- http://www.historyforkids.org/
- http://www.kidspast.com/world-history/0102 civilizations-of-india.php
- http://www.indianchild.com/history_of_india.htm
- http://www.mapsofindia.com/history/
- http://www.indhistory.com/
- http://www.webindia123.com/history/
- http://www.kamat.com/kalranga/timeline/ timeline.htm
- http://www.bbc.co.uk/history/ancient/india/
- http://www.kidspast.com/world-history/0102- civilizations-of-india.php
- http://homeschooling.gomilpitas.com/explore/ india.htm

World History:

- http://www.kidspast.com/world-history/index.php
- http://worldhistory.mrdonn.org/
- http://www.socialstudiesforkids.com/subjects/ worldhistorygeneral.htm
- http://www.kidsclick.org/midhist.html
- http://www.abookintime.com/history-games/ world-history-games.html
- http://www.pitara.com/reference/history/
- http://www.kidsites.com/sites-edu/history.htm
- http://www.funtrivia.com/quizzes/for_children/ topics_for_kids/history_for_kids.html
- http://www.mrdonn.org/ancienthistory.html

- http://www.wartgames.com/themes/world history.html

Books for Children

The following is only a sampling of the many excellent books about people, events, and issues in Indian and world history and geography that your child might enjoy. Many of the books listed here are also available in languages other than English. Your local or school librarian can help you locate books in a particular language.

We have given here the books for those most appropriate for you to read with your younger child and for those that will appeal to your older child, who reads independently. However, you're the best judge of which books are appropriate for your child, regardless of age.

Indian History:

- *I Used to Know That: History*: Emma Marriott, Michael O Mara Books, 2010, 192 p, ISBN : 9781843174752

- *Legends from Indian History*: A.K. Ghosh, CBT Publication, 64 pages, ISBN 81-7011-046-7.

- *A Pinch of Salt Rocks an Empire*: Sarojini Sinha, CBT Publication, 88 pages, ISBN 81-7011-291-5.

- *An Earthquake the Bastar Rebellion*: Loveleen

Kacker, CBT Publication, 128 pps., ISBN 81-7011-909-X.

- *Indira Priyadarshini*: Alaka Shankar, CBT Publication, 144 pages, ISBN 81-7011-357-1.

- *Nehru for Children*: M. Chalapathi Rau, CBT Publication, 112 pages, ISBN 81-7011-035-1.

- *The Story of Gandhi*: Rajkumari Shankar, CBT Publication, 124 pages, ISBN 81-7011-064-5.

World History:

- *The Story of the World: History for the Classical Child, Volume 1: Ancient Times*: Bauer, Susan Wise, Peace Hill Press.

- *Mummies of the Pharaohs: Exploring the Valley of the Kings*: Berger, Melvin and Berger, Gilda, National Geographic Society.

- *Black Potatoes: The Story of the Great Irish Famine*: Bartoletti, Susan Campbell, 1845-1850, Houghton Mifflin.

- *Pyramid of the Sun, Pyramid of the Moon*: Fisher, Leonard E. Atheneum.

- *Emperors and Gladiators*: Ganeri, Anita, Peter Bedrick Books.

- *Ashanti to Zulu: African Traditions*: Musgrove, Margaret W. Dial Books for Young Readers.

- *The Glorious Flight: Across the Channel with Louis Blériot*: Provensen, Alice and Provensen, Martin, Puffin.

- *A to Zen: A Book of Japanese Culture*: Wells, Ruth, Simon & Schuster.

- *The Colors of Russia*: Zimlicka, Shannon, Carolrhoda Books.

Understand Your Child: Teen and Child Personality Test

http://www.personalitylab.org/tests/ccq_ parent_ choose.htm